This book belongs to

_____

Henry Holt and Company, LLC
PUBLISHERS SINCE 1866
175 Fifth Avenue
New York, New York 10010
www.HenryHoltKids.com

Henry Holt® is a registered trademark of Henry Holt and Company, LLC.
Copyright © 2007 by Sam Lloyd
First published in the United States in 2008 by Henry Holt and Company, LLC
Originally published in England in 2007 by Orchard Books
All rights reserved.
Distributed in Canada by H. B. Fenn and Company Ltd.

Library of Congress Control Number: 2007938928
ISBN-13: 978-0-8050-8819-9
ISBN-10: 0-8050-8819-9

First American Edition—2008
Printed in Singapore on acid-free paper. ∞

1 3 5 7 9 10 8 6 4 2

Kiss-it-Better Hospital

Doctor Meow's BIG EMERGENCY

Sam Lloyd

Henry Holt and Company
New York

It's another bright morning
at Kiss-it-Better Hospital.
Outside, Woof is busy cleaning
the blue light on his ambulance.

Inside, Doctor Meow is very busy.
There are lots of patients for
her to look after!

Mr. Crocodile

He has come
out in a nasty
rash from
something
he ate.

Horse Ned

His heart
skipped a beat
when he did
his high jump.

There are temperatures to take, heartbeats
to listen to, baby bunnies to feed, and look at
Monkey—what's he got stuck on his head this
time? My goodness, so much to do!

And now the phone is ringing!!

"Hello," says Doctor Meow. "This is Kiss-it-Better Hospital. How can we help?"

"Meooooow! It's Tom Cat. I've fallen out of the apple tree and hurt myself. Please come quickly!"

"We'll be there right away!"
says Doctor Meow.

Doctor Meow dashes outside.
"Quick, Woof! Tom Cat has had an accident and we must help him!"

"I'll start the engine," says Woof. "Let's go!"
They climb into the ambulance and off they zoom!

Wee-ooo, wee-ooo goes the siren.
"Faster, Woof! Faster!" says Doctor Meow.
"Turn left here."

Wee-ooo, wee-ooo, wee-ooo, wee-ooo,

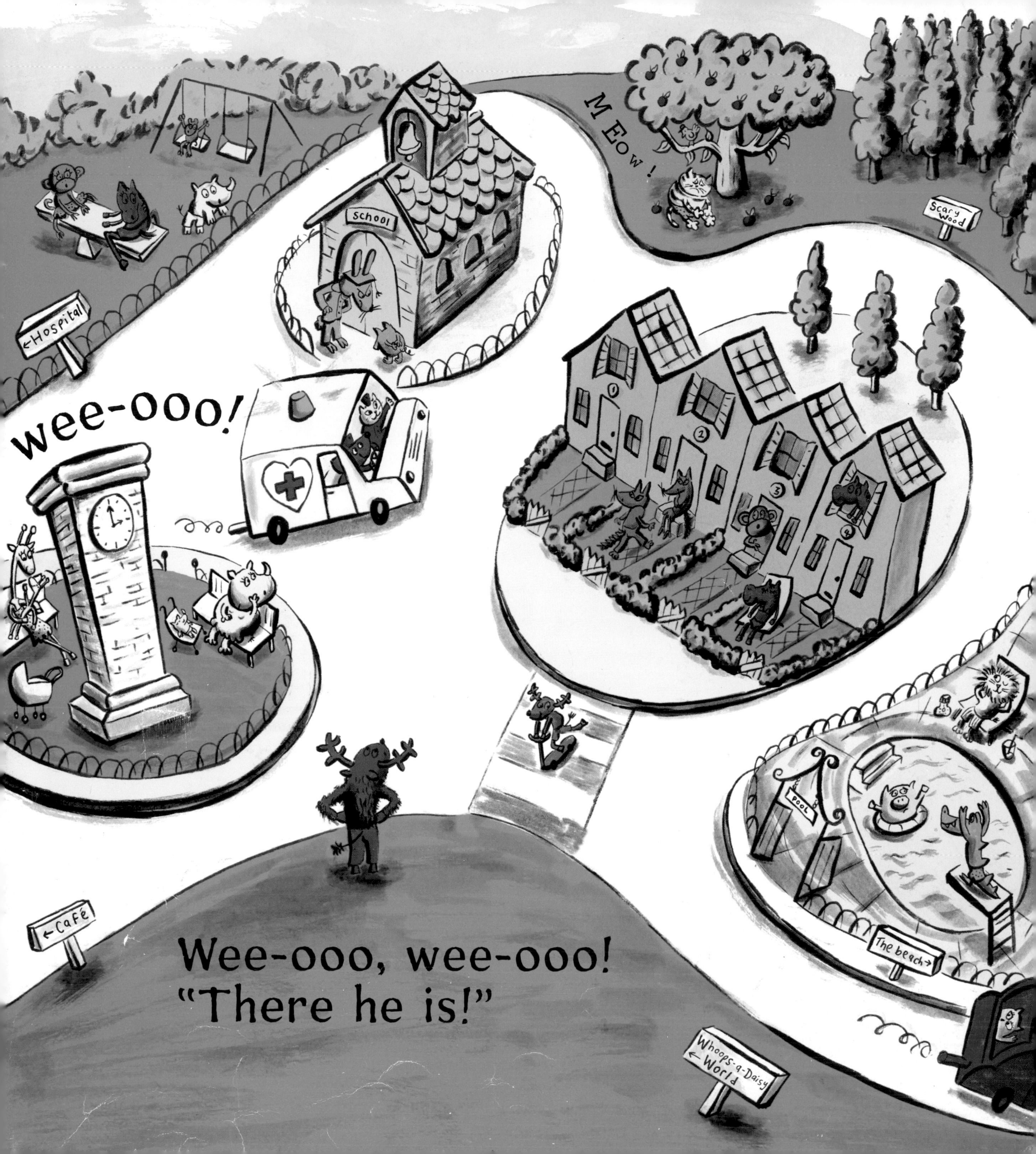

Wee-ooo, wee-ooo!
"There he is!"

Doctor Meow races over to Tom Cat.
"My leg hurts," he sobs.
Doctor Meow gently examines it.
"How did this happen?" she asks.
"I was chasing Mr. Bird up the tree
and I slipped," cries Tom Cat.

"I think your leg is broken," says Doctor Meow. "You'll have to go to the hospital."

Doctor Meow and Woof carefully put Tom Cat on a stretcher and whisk him off to the ambulance...

...and Woof drives back to
Kiss-it-Better Hospital as quickly
as he can. Wee-ooo, wee-ooo!

Back at the hospital, Doctor Meow takes an X-ray of Tom Cat's broken leg. Then she puts a very special cast on it to make it better.

"You shouldn't chase Mr. Bird," says Doctor Meow. "He's a lot smaller than you." Tom Cat feels sorry.

"Oh dear," sighs Tom Cat. "I've hurt my leg, but I've hurt poor Mr. Bird's feelings more. I hope he'll still be my friend."

But cheer up, Tom Cat, you've got a visitor!

Rat-a-tat-tat!

There's a knock at the door...

It's Mr. Bird!

"I'm sorry I was mean to you,"
says Tom Cat.
"That's okay," says Mr. Bird.
"Let's be friends again."
"Hooray!" cheers Tom Cat.

"Would you like to sign my cast?" asks Tom Cat.